Football Fumble

Adaptation by Karen Barss
Based on a TV series teleplay written by Raye Lankford
Based on the characters created by Susan Meddaugh

HOUGHTON MIFFLIN HARCOURT
Boston • New York

AGES	GRADES	GUIDED READING LEVEL	READING RECOVERY LEVEL	LEXILE® LEVEL
5–7	1	I	15–16	150L

For information about permission to reproduce selections from this book, write to Permissions, Houghton Mifflin Harcourt, 215 Park Avenue South, New York, New York 10003.
ISBN: 978-0-544-08902-0 pa
ISBN: 978-0-544-08764-4 pob

Design by Rebecca Bond
www.hmhbooks.com
www.marthathetalkingdog.com
Manufactured in China
SCP 10 9 8 7 6 5 4 3 2 1
4500420034

Helen and her friends play football.
Their team is called the Wagstaff Dogs.
They lost their game today.
Again.
The final score was 77 to 2.

The team feels down.
Carolina tries to cheer them up.

"It isn't your fault," she says.
"Your coach called bad plays."
"We don't have a coach," T.D. says.

"Too bad," Carolina says.
"You could win with a good coach."
"You think so?" T.D. says.
"Sure," she says.
"I know a lot about football."

Then Carolina sees her friends.
"Ew, a ball!" Carolina says.
She drops the football.
The girls wave and walk by.

"I can't help you," Carolina says.
"I love football.
But it's not girly."

"But the team needs you!" Martha says.

The Wagstaff Dogs do not give up.
The next day they go to Carolina's.
They beg her for help.
Finally, she says yes.

"I can teach you all the plays.
But you can't tell anyone!" she says.

Carolina is a good coach.
The team runs drills every day.

They learn to pass, catch, and kick.
Soon they are ready . . .

As ready as they can be!

It is the day of the big game.
The Wildcats look tough.
But where is Carolina?
The Wagstaff Dogs have no coach!
Without Carolina, things look bad.

Truman's kickoff rolls two feet.

The Wildcats grab the ball.
They score.

At halftime the team finds Carolina.
"We need you!" T.D. says.
"I can't! My friends might see me."
"But you're our coach!" Helen says.
"And you look cute in plaid!"

I have a plan!

Carolina comes to the game.
She hides so no one will see her.
She tells Martha the plays.
Then Martha tells the team.

The team follows Carolina's plays.
They move down the field.
But T.D. fumbles!
The Wildcats get the ball.
Time is running out!

The Wagstaff Dogs are glum.
They huddle up.
"We gave it our best shot," they say.
Then they hear Coach Carolina:
"TIME OUT!" she yells.

"This is your last game this year.
Don't give up.
No matter what,
you are winners in my eyes.
Go get 'em!" she says.

The team takes the field.
The Wildcats pass the ball . . .

Helen intercepts it!
She throws it to T.D.

He makes a touchdown!
The score is tied 6 to 6!

All eyes are on Truman.
The team holds their breath.
He kicks . . .

. . . and he SCORES!
Everybody cheers.

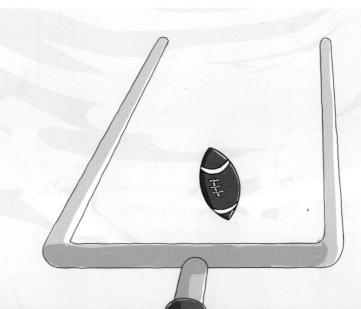

The Wagstaff Dogs win!

Then Carolina sees her friends.
Uh-oh, she thinks. *Busted.*
"Great game, Coach!" they say.
"You look so cute in plaid."